# MAX THE GORILLA

By: K.A. Mulenga

© Kalenga Augustine Mulenga

MAX THE GORILLA

Published by Kalenga Augustine Mulenga

Johannesburg, South Africa

augustine@kamulenga.com

ISBN: 978-1-998954-40-7

eISBN: 978-1-998954-41-4

2 4 6 8 10 9 7 5 3 1

All rights reserved. No part of this publication may be reproduced, stored in a retrieval system, or transmitted in any form by any means electronic, mechanical, photocopying, recording or otherwise without the written permission of the copyright owner.

Illustration and layout by Boutique Books

Printed in South Africa by Bidvest Data

*I dedicate this book to my wife Sheba and my kids, Grace, Malaika and Kalenga Jr.*

*Thank you for believing in me!*

*Thank you to Pamela Nomvete, whose generosity has funded the publication of this book.*

A long time ago, a gorilla called Max was born in a zoo in Germany, called the Frankfurt Zoo. The people who were looking after him decided he would be happier living in South Africa, so they transported him to the Johannesburg Zoo.

Max lived in the zoo with his wife, Lisa. Children loved going to the zoo and watching Max and Lisa, playing, eating and happily going about their gorilla business.

One day, Max did something amazing, which made him instantly famous!

Max and his wife had enjoyed their evening meal and were preparing to go to bed when, suddenly, a man jumped into their enclosure. The man was a robber and was being hotly pursued by four policemen.

The robber swam across the safety moat around Max's enclosure ... and there he met Max!

The robber was shaking in his boots, and Max was not happy that he and Lisa had been disturbed. In fact, he was furious! He attacked the robber. The robber tried to fight back, but he was no match for Max. After intense wrestling, the robber lay prostrate as a result of Max's combat.

The police came into the enclosure and handcuffed the robber. Off to jail he went.

'Silly robber,' Max thought to himself 'that will teach you a lesson! Do not disturb a gorilla when he is about to go to bed!'

'My hero,' thought Lisa, looking at Max lovingly.

The people at the zoo were so proud of Max for his bravery that they decided to build a statue of him.

So, if you go to the Johannesburg Zoo today, make sure you look out for the statue of Max the Gorilla at the gorilla enclosure to this day. Max was a true hero!

# THE END

### By K.A. Mulenga

Chuck the Cheetah

David, the great king

Donk and the Stubborn Donkeys

Elaine the Elephant

Four seasons in one day

Harry the Honest Horse

Imbwa, the Story Of the Dog and His Harsh Master

Joe Finds His Way Home

Max the Gorilla

Polly the Polecat

Robbie the Raven and Debbie the Dove

Spike and Spud , the Spaceboys

Susie Strickland, Sizzling Striker

The Leopard Licks Its Spots

The Lion and the Impala

The Weaver Birds

Will and His Best Friend Whale

Thank you for reading Max the Gorilla. I hope you enjoyed it! Please let K.A. Mulenga know about what you thought about the book by leaving a short review on Amazon, it will help other parents and children find the story.
(If you're under 13, ask a grown up to help you)

**Top Tip**: Be sure not to give away any of the story's secrets!

---

Sign up to my readers' club weekly newsletter.
Simply click on the YES, SIGN ME UP button on my website.
I will never share your email address. Unsubscribe at any time.